What if?

FRAN LEWIS

Table of Contents

What if?

One Race: One World

THE YEAR 2050

The world has really changed by 2050. There were no more planes or trains. All you needed to do was think about being somewhere and you were there. The government, in order to save money on gas and fuel, had banned cars, buses, and any means of transportation, and implanted chips in everyone's arms that helped transport them to wherever they wanted to go, including the past.

A huge explosion had occurred, and all that was left in the world were twenty countries, with only twelve hundred people in each country. Most people had not survived the explosion, which had caused most of the countries to just disappear into space forever. No one really knew if anyone was out there or if these people survived somewhere, and no one really cared enough to find out.

One man called The Ruler headed all the countries, and assigned one person as the Chief of Law and Enforcement in each country. Under this person, five people helped to enforce the rules and the laws.

Then, one miserable day, someone decided there were too many wars, too many hate crimes, too many people being killed on the streets, and too much traffic and congestion on the highways. The government hired several scientists to find a solution to the problem, and that was how everyone in the entire world wound up multicolored.

Because of all the wars and fighting and hate that took place in the past, the government created a way to eliminate the many different races in the world and opted for only one. Everyone looked the same. Our faces might have looked a little different, but our skin colors were the same—multicolored. They did this so that no one would insult, mock, or hurt anyone because of their skin color. They eliminated houses of worship so that everyone was nonsectarian, and no one would be discriminated against. However, what they could not eliminate were our thoughts and desires to make changes in our lives, even though they tried.

Everyone that lived here had a job that paid the same amount. No one, no matter what they did or what career they chose, was paid more than anyone else. We never had to worry about being laid off. Unless we decided to move somewhere else our job stayed the same, and there was no room for advancement—ever. Everyone did the same thing every day. Nothing changed. Life was supposed to be anger free, insult free, and most of all, calm and tranquil. HOW DULL AND BORING! (OH! I am not supposed to say that. Opinions are not allowed here.)

One morning I got up and got dressed to go to my boring job as an accountant with the only accounting firm in this city. I went over the books daily, entered my accounts in their daily ledgers, and did taxes for some of the companies in this city. It was grunt work, and nothing exciting ever happened at work or anywhere else.

Walking to work as usual, I began remembering how it was only twenty years ago when there were cars, trains, and people running and yelling for cabs and trains to wait for them at the station. I missed the newspaper people on the street and the vendors selling hot coffee and bagels from their pushcarts. Those were the days. I loved the way people had looked and the different races and nationalities that lived here. Learning from other people was what made life exciting.

Then the unexpected happened. A new family with two children moved in down the street from me. These two kids were not going to conform to our way of thinking, and decided it was time to shake things up—and they did. One morning when going to school they each wore something other than the school's drab gray uniform. The girl wore a pink and green dress with flowers, and the boy wore something blue, and a shirt that said, "I hate being the same. Different Rules."

This did not go over well, and they were taken into custody by the guards in their school and promptly suspended. This did not stop them.

They started screaming and yelling all sorts of words we had not heard before. "One race is not what we are supposed to be. I hate this planet. I hate all of you."

I could not believe my ears. This was grounds for banishment into the Devoid Zone. These two children had painted stars all over their faces. Their younger sister decided to paint her face one color. Who in today's world had a face that was one color? Everyone here looked and dressed the same. It prevented jealousy, arguments, and fashion wars. How dare they go against the laws of this state?

Walking to school they had met several of their friends, who just ran away from them. They were afraid of what might happen to them if they were seen with anyone that was different. Kids were not supposed to make any decisions, and neither should the adults.

The person in charge of handling this case was the police chief, who had a force of about twenty-five officers for the entire country. This was the first time a serious crime had been committed where banishment might be the final sentence for these children and their parents. It was not that people didn't steal or try to hurt others, but for the most part in this country, where nothing changed and our days and nights were exactly the same, it was rare that the police were needed.

Police Chief Robbie got the call from one of his officers who had spotted the two children running down the street, yelling, "Down with being the same. Different is in. This is stupid. I want to dress the way I want and not the anyone tells me to." This would never do. They could not be allowed to think for themselves. What would happen if everyone in all the twenty countries decided to change things? What would happen if everyone in these countries decided to think for him or herself?

Police Chief Robbie and three of his officers arrested the entire family that night. These people would ruin their perfect country. Just think: Children would start to ask questions in school. Children might learn from other kids the right things, and maybe even the wrong things, to do. Cars and buses might be brought back, and then there would be too much pollution and noise.

I loved having the chip in my arm, just thinking about where I wanted to go and instantly getting there. If everyone looked different and people had a voice in the government, there would be wars, fighting, and arguing, and the world would go back to what it was before the mass explosion.

You decide: How do we get a little of both? Wars are horrible and everyone gets hurt on both sides. Hate is awful, and no one wins.

What do you think? Just think—2050 is not too far away.

Crime Pays Off

JUST DON'T GET CAUGHT!

The year was 2020, and I was sitting on a couch in a plain room, with nothing but four blank walls staring me in the face. Things were different now. Buildings had no windows, fresh air was pumped in through vents, cars were battery operated, and the outside world did not exist for me.

I am Harold, and I am fifty years old and a genius. I understand the market, playing the horses, slots, and any game of chance. I can tell you how to beat the odds at a roulette table. I can even teach you how to count cards in blackjack.

I was the sole founder and owner of an Internet company,

www.JustAskHaroldAndHeWillTellYou.com.

People from everywhere in the world would email me, text me, and call for advice on just about every subject. I controlled the markets and told stockbrokers which stocks were hot, which were cold. I gave advice to rich executives who needed to make investments in order to liquidate funds and get some quick cash. My clients made millions, and so did I. For a monthly fee and a large commission, these rich executives were able to make these investments, and no one knew where or how they were made. Hidden bank accounts were untraceable, and everyone was happy, especially me.

Starting the company and creating the website was easy. Advertising on YouTube, Facebook, and other sites helped to get the word out that I was there to help anyone who had money to invest, and needed to do it quickly and quietly without the knowledge of the IRS or anyone else in government.

So why was I sitting in a room with four walls, locked away, never to see the outside world again? Because somehow, someway, I was caught.

Sitting there contemplating my fate I began to see flashes of things to come; or were they? Looking at the wall, I saw a man who looked just like me, but it was not me. He had a wife and family and looked well off. Then the vision disappeared.

I began thinking of what I should do next. There were no windows or doors in the room where I was, and the only contact I had with people was through a small vent in the ceiling. Prisons were now escape proof, and once locked away there was no way out. All my belongings had been taken from me when I was placed in this room. It was not my final stop or where I would remain for the rest of my sorry and miserable life. It was called the Limbo Room, where you stayed until you figured out what would happen next—or they did it for you.

Sitting at the small desk in the room, I began to see some more of the vision from before. I saw this man at work, and I wanted to learn more about his life and what he did. I saw him sitting behind a large desk in an office with plush carpeting and huge bay windows, with a cappuccino machine and his own beautiful young secretary.

Wearing a black suit, steel grey shirt, and tie, he looked polished and ready for whatever he was supposed to be doing. Then the vision disappeared, and I saw the blank wall in front of me.

I was a mogul of industry. Presidents of countries would use my website to help them make major oil deals, whether to purchase companies or to get weapons for their armies to fight other countries. I was paid handsomely, and never discussed my clients with anyone.

I worked alone except for a small staff of people that watched the markets in every country for me, checked oil prices around the world, and dealt with those in charge of selling weapons that were needed by my major clients. None of these people ever left their offices to go home.

Everyone lived in the building where my company was, and everyone was carefully investigated and had to sign some special forms swearing never to divulge what they did to anyone before being hired. Any outside friends or family were not told what they did, nor did they have any contact with these people if they worked for me.

Therefore, how was I caught, and what was my downfall? Why did I think my life was so great? It was not now, and they would be coming for me soon. I was not going to remain in Limbo much longer. However, I had to figure out who this man was and what he had to do with my future.

Time moved slowly. I was sitting facing the back wall, and this time the vision was clearer. I could hear voices and what people were saying. This man's name was also Harold, and he was a bank president with a wife, two children, and a girlfriend.

He was not only the president of the bank, but he controlled what investments the money in the bank was used for and where the profits went. I heard him on the phone with the CFO and the CEO of the bank discussing a possible takeover of another bank. He began to get worried and did not like what he was hearing. Harold liked things the way they were, and did not like these two men interfering with the bank's daily operations. Nor did he want this bank takeover.

The vision disappeared again, but now I had some idea where I might fit in and how I might not be in Limbo forever. However, I needed to learn more about this man and who he was, where he lived, and how his life would make mine better. Staring at the wall, I hoped to see something. However, I did not.

I heard a voice from the vent, saying, "Harold, you have twenty-four hours to go, and then your fate will be decided. Do you understand?"

I did not bother to answer. It did not require a response. They could read my mind, and if they did, they would not like what they heard. However, give up I would not, and focus and concentrate I would.

I was never satisfied with my life. I was never happy until I created my Internet company, and even then, I was dissatisfied. Not very handsome and never really noticed when walking on the street, I decided to make myself more marketable and more noticeable by starting the company and helping people get rich.

I was getting tired, but I could not sleep—my survival depended on figuring out who this man was and why he was important to me. The vision was clearer now. I saw him at home with his wife and family. He had dinner, went into his study, and made several calls. I could hear what he was saying. "I need you to take five million dollars and invest it for me in Company A. I then need you to take five million more and invest it in Company B. When you are done and the money is where I want it and the investments are made, I want you to sell both off.

"No, you do not use company money; you use the money in the client funds, and make sure you tell no one. My wife wants a new car, my girls want to go on several trips, and I want to make it happen. Do whatever you have to do to get those investments made, and make sure when the stocks go up you sell them and electronically transfer the money into my special account. The clients? Well, they will be none the wiser.

"Do not record any of this in their portfolios and do not discuss this with anyone. Remember, you owe me, and I can destroy you with one phone call."

The vision went away, but the man in the room and what he was doing was no different from what I had done—but he had not been caught. He was using client money to fund his own investments. His wife had inherited a lot of money from an aunt that died, and he had embezzled all of it for his own purposes. She had no idea. If he kept her happy and gave her whatever she wanted, she would never question what he was doing with her money or where it was going.

As he sat there waiting for the phone call his cell phone rang. It was his secretary girlfriend, who he wanted to dump. She was becoming too demanding and wanted a permanent position in his life, and he had it too good at this time and was not going to make any changes just yet.

The vision disappeared and the voice coming from the vent said, "You have five more hours and then it is over." I felt my body shake and hoped the vision would appear one more time so I would know the outcome, and what I had to get out of Limbo.

Staring straight at the wall, I began to feel a little strange. My arms started to tingle, and I felt faint. Since there was just a small cot for me to rest on, I had no choice but to lie down on the hard metal floor. I started to shiver and shake all over. I could not stop. What had they put in my lunch? What had they put through the air vent? Was this the end, or was it something else? Maybe I was not going to escape my fate. Maybe this was where I would spend eternity for what I had done.

After a few minutes, the shaking stopped, and I felt better. I heard the voice say, "Four more hours and then…." Looking straight at the wall, I could hear the man speaking, and knew that all was about to be revealed. The voice coming out of the vent in my cell said, "Listen carefully, Harold. You will hear this only once and see it in a flash. Remember all details, or you will lose and go somewhere much worse than Limbo. Heed my warning."

I looked at the man in the vision and studied his mannerisms and what he was doing. I heard him say the same things to people that I said before being caught. "Do not worry. That new shipment of cars with the hybrid engines was already sent with the extra packages in the trunks." "Do not worry. We obtained the stocks you wanted to purchase, and they will be worth twice as much in the morning." "Do not worry, Mr. President, no one will know." "Do not worry, Mr. Ambassador, I will never tell."

Then suddenly, I realized something. All my life I was smart. All my life I did the right thing and towed the mark. I helped all these people get rich, using every trick and every get rich quick method I knew. So, why was I here? I was just a plain and ordinary man. I had never complained about my life, dull as it was. Even though I made others rich, and myself too, it became routine and boring after a while. I guess I gave someone the wrong tip or gave the wrong person a good stock tip.

Here it was—the final vision. It was now or never to find out what I must do. Staring straight at the man I saw and heard him quite clearly. While sitting behind his huge oak desk and dictating a letter to someone, his cell phone rang. Listening to the person on the end we both heard the same thing. The man's face turned white. He dropped the phone on the floor and just stared at the door in front of him. The person on the phone had told him that he would pay for what he did. He said the tip the man had given him cost the caller everything and more. This was Harold's end.

Time seemed to race ahead, and the next thing I knew the voice coming from the vent said, "You have been here ten years and it is now 2030, and your time in Limbo is up. Did you figure it out yet? You have had all this time to learn what you need to do to get out. Look ahead and see your fate, or remain…."

The man in the vision was now in a room just like mine, chained to the chair. Three people were in the room interrogating him. "I swear I never smuggled drugs or sold rare gems to foreign leaders. I never embezzled money from my clients or stole from their portfolios. I never took gave bad stock tips.

I invested in the same things they did and in the same companies. I even gave them shares in my company. I watched how he did it all those years. I kept a close eye on everything he did. I am even using his website:

www.JustAskHaroldAndHeWillTellYou.com.

did not change anything. I even had my surgeon make me look like him. I hated him all my life, and I still hate him. I was the one who everyone thought would amount to nothing. I was the one who followed the rules and never got in trouble. How could this happen? I am just a fifty-year-old investment counselor who got caught up in the frenzy."

Listening to them speak I realized what I had to do, and I hoped it would work. Staring straight at the wall and watching what looked like a live video feed from an interrogation room, I saw the three men turn the man to face the wall and tell him to walk toward it, and not to stop when he came face to face with it. As he walked toward the wall, I walked in the direction of the wall that was facing me.

The next thing I knew I was sitting with his wife and family in his house in his chair. He was now where I used to be, in Limbo or worse. I was now him and he was now me. This time, I would do things to help those that needed stock tips, investments, and more—BUT THIS TIME I WOULD *NOT* GET CAUGHT!

I even set up a new, untraceable website:

www.IdDidIt_ha-ha.com

Visit the site and ask me anything.

The Match

I light the match and drop it into the fireplace.
I see the smoke billowing; I can feel the heat on
    my face.
I see the match turning into ash, you see,
No longer able to ignite no longer able to
    provide heat for me.

It is cold outside, and the cabin is chilled.
I am stuck inside due to a snowstorm, in which
    many were buried or killed.
The snow has closed the highways and the lights
    are out.
There is no way for anyone to rescue me, I have
    no doubt.

I have two more matches and one large candle
    to help me keep warm,

But as I look through the window, I begin to see
the outline of a form.
I do not know what it is, and I see it coming
closer to the cabin door.
It could be a bear, a deer, or worse—someone
that I want to see no more.

I have no lights, and I hide in the other room so
my face in the firelight does not show.
I see him enter the cabin, and his face frightens
me, you know.
I have no weapon, and I have no one to protect
me from harm or worse.
All I can find is something sharp in the bottom
of my purse.

Standing near the burning fire I see his face
quite clear.
I know I am in trouble because it is him that I
fear.
I came here to sort out my feelings and more.
I could not stand the unhappiness each day had
in store.

I hope and pray that he does not decide to stay
here all night.
I hope that he does not decide to search the
cabin or notice my cup that I left in plain
sight.
The snow has subsided, and I start to hear the
plows coming up my path.
Hoping they get here so I do not have to deal
with his wrath.

As he hears the snowplows coming closer you
see,
He turns around and comes closer to the door,
opens it, and finds me.
I hold this sharp object pointed directly at him,
and pray
That he does not come closer, because I will
protect myself in every way.

Looking straight into my eyes he sees the anger
and fear.
Looking straight into my eyes he does not see a
tear.

Turning around, he hears someone shout out
    and call.
He runs out of the cabin, and down a large slope
    he falls.

I come out the room and light another match.
I hope that whoever called out will catch
Him before it is too late because I know he is
    not hurt.
He fell down a large slope and into some solid
    dirt.

He is a mountain climber and hunter, and a
    man people fear.
I slowly close the cabin door and stand by to
    hear.
I get closer to the fire and hopefully will stay
    warm.
Hoping that I will no longer have to see his
    form.

The Pharmacist

Deep within the gated forest, hidden beneath a huge plaque, was an underground pharmacy filled with tubes, applicators, printers, cables, adapters, and a wide range of accessories. Capsule machines included everything from pill counters and tampers to full system packages. Clean room products such as air samplers, protective clothing, and cleaning products were available, including hoods and accessories and base stands, HEPA filters, work surfaces, and more. Finally, there were mixing, milling, and filling products.

The drug compounding done in this pharmacy was the process of combining, mixing, or altering ingredients to create medication specifically needed for an individual patient. It included the combining of two or more drugs which were not FDA approved. The unique compounds or formulations were often vital to meet a patient's needs. When a person was allergic to an inactive ingredient found in a commercially available form of the medication, a special compound would be needed—but remember, the special formulations were not FDA approved. Compounded drugs were prepared according to a unique recipe that combined, mixed, or altered ingredients in order to meet the patient's needs.

The pharmacist in charge was me, MD, a licensed pharmacist specially trained in the field of compound pharmacy to understand the many chemicals used to meet the individual patient needs. Some patients could not swallow pills, and others could not use a spoon for liquid medication. Others might need an ointment or some other way to get their medication. If they could not swallow a pill MD might be able to create a compound that would provide the drug in liquid form.

This apothecary was a place few knew about it. Buried beneath the plaque in the forest was my pharmacy, and only two others had access to it, and only on a limited basis. These two could pre-pare medications that did not require too many ingredients, then show them to me and explain exactly how the drug was prepared. There was no room for mistakes.

Patients were admitted one a time by appointment only. Proper identification, a prescription, and their doctor's credentials and contact number were required. Because this was not a regular pharmacy insurance was handled differently. I was receiving a shipment of chemicals and other equipment needed to fill the prescriptions.

It should be noted that most prescription medications, over the counter medications, and nutritional supplements contain inactive or inert ingredients in addition to the active ones. Unfortunately, some powders could be tainted. Others might have the right expiration date on the bottle for a new med, but expired powders were placed in the bottle instead. It was also easy to switch labels for one drug with another, and no one would be the wiser unless they knew what the compound powder should look like.

All prescriptions were sent electronically so there was no mistake about what should be prepared. But in this case, I was not made aware of the patient's allergies because none were listed on the profile or written anywhere by the prescribing doctor. However, I did contact the doctor's office and was told this person had no allergies to any medications. The compounds were delivered, and I checked the labels, and as far as I knew they were correctly labeled. Each one specified how to create the correct formula for the medication needed, how to add other ingredients, and had a picture of what each medication should look like in liquid or pill form. Each medication was a specific color and shape, and the proper dosages and quantities were on each bottle. So, how could mistakes be made?

I refrigerated those required to be refrigerated, and locked up the pills and ointments and salves, labeling the outer door of the place where they were stored so that I would not have to rummage through the contents of each one to find what I needed. I thought I had everything stored and locked in place.

My apartment was at the back end of this apothecary. I rarely ventured outdoors or anywhere else. The lab was not seen or known by anyone except those delivering supplies, which never came to the front door that was hidden beneath the bushes and under a flat gravestone carved with the name of a deceased person, so it appeared to be a marker and not exactly what it was.

Like all hospitals, or in this case my apothecary, I had a chute that was used for the deliveries, but since this was a secret place I could not divulge where the chute was. Just suffice it to say it was in a place where no one else would find it except the one person I trusted—my assistant, who pushed the supplies down the chute when he was not working in the lab.

So, how did Mr. H and Mr. R get the wrong medicine? How did one get a formula that had sulfur in it, and the other with penicillin? At first I had no idea, until I realized that someone might have switched the label on the penicillin with that of one that was the same liquid color but had added sulfur in it. But why?

The company that sent the medicines, the liquids, and whatever I needed to compose the compounds had been in business for quite some time. Something about the last batch seemed odd, and yet I never suspected that they would purposely mislabel the ingredients in order to harm my patients. One of the techs that worked for me was responsible for cataloging all the bottles, placing them on the correct shelves, and labeling what they were and what they were used for. He had been here a short time, which led me to do a search on him hoping to learn more about his qualifications. The company that sent the ingredients sent him to me with a glowing recommendation. Could they be behind this, along with him, in order to take the apothecary away from me and give it to someone they wanted in order to make a profit?

Things began to get even worse when I got an email from the FDA stating that someone was going to come and check things out firsthand. How did they even know I existed and where I was located? Was it really the FDA? And who was this person that was coming to check on my medications and ingredients firsthand? A phone call to the FDA, using the name and address of the person on the email, told me that this was bogus, and someone would check into it. But when they called me back something still sounded off. It was like someone had tampered with my phone lines, and the call was coming from somewhere else. I checked the caller ID and it read unknown and no number, which led me to believe the person might have blocked their number—or maybe there was some other reason for this call.

I never answered unknown numbers—I usually waited until they left a voice message, and this caller did. The message gave a number in Washington, and not knowing exactly where the FDA was, I hesitated to call them, not wanting to unblock my number. A little research showed that the FDA had its headquarters in unincorporated White Oak, Maryland, and had 223 field offices and thirteen laboratories throughout the United States, the Virgin Islands, and Puerto Rico. Looking up the area codes for these places and hoping to match one, the number from the message did not come up—but I did discover that the number given to me was an area code in China.

Calling the FDA on their Maryland number, I informed them that my apothecary was having an issue; that someone was playing with the ingredients, the labels were switched, and people were getting sick, and I needed them to investigate the companies that were sending me my supplies. After speaking with the FDA, I learned that it was their responsibility to protect public health by regulating human drugs and biologics, animal drugs, medical devices, tobacco products, food—including animal food—electronic products that emit radiation, and cosmetics. It had a wide spectrum of responsibilities, and I imagined that they had overseers, checks and balances to make sure that each area was properly monitored, and that the drugs were tested and got FDA approval after their tests proved that the drugs, for either animals or humans, were safe. But something happened with my compounds and ingredients and the FDA was not responsible for these compounds. I knew that penicillin and other drugs were FDA approved, so what was I to do? Who was playing games with my patients' lives, and why? Someone wanted me out, but who and why?

Thinking back to before I established this apothecary, I remembered an assistant that worked with me at another pharmacy. At times I had thought I miscounted some of the meds I ordered and had filled. I knew each drug had a specific amount you could reorder to replenish your supply based on the prescriptions filled. Some of the opioids seemed to have been prescribed over the limit, and when checking the prescriptions and backtracking the doctors who called them in, I could not find the names, license numbers, or any office address in the medical directory. This led me to believe that someone had called in from a burner phone, listed the names of these doctors that I finally realized did exist, and used old prescriptions that had all of their information and even their license numbers on them, because this person had someone in each office that was profiting from helping with this. But how could I prove this, and how did this person get into my apothecary? Or was this one of my suppliers and I just did not know it?

I decided to place an order that would be over the limit and see where it got me asking the name and phone number of the contact person at this company, hoping to learn how this was done. Someone did answer my request with an email and a name, calling himself Tom with no last name. I asked for a phone number and none came. What pharmacy or company are you with, and how do I get delivery? When I received no direct information or response or identification, I began thinking that I might have to inform some type of law enforcement, but I hesitated. Not sure who to trust and who might have access to my information, I thought I was protected. I had every security and firewall on my computers, and even had padlocks on every cabinet in my apothecary—and I had the only key. No one prepared anything but me, and I dispensed the drugs in a secretive manner that no one really knew about.

Someone somehow was pretending to be me and ordering drugs over the limit, and the pharmaceutical companies should have contacted me in order to find out why. Not one hour later I received another call from someone named Bill, who claimed to have received my order for another opioid and wanted to know just how many pills I needed and stated that amount was no problem. Once again asking for identification and wondering how these people had located me, the only thing I could think of was my cell phone. Without my realizing it my number came up on their screen but with no name, and some-how, they hacked into the system to find me, hoping to get a substantial order for these drugs and over charge me, making it seem as if the pharmaceutical company they worked for was increasing the price according to the amount I ordered. Things got even more tense when I went to where I received my medications, and found triple the amount I had ordered, with a note say-ing I had better fill the prescriptions for the peo-ple listed on the pad left inside of the boxes. Fear set in, as I had no idea who had left this note, why these people would need these pain pills, or the enormous amount of money I would get for filling all these prescriptions.

Someone wanted to turn my apothecary into a pill mill, and apparently someone I worked with before had decided to threaten me if I did not comply. I had no idea what I was going to do, but I did not want to be involved with filling prescriptions for people who went to a pill mill. They had probably already seen a doctor who wrote a legal prescription, but in addition to filling it in a pharmacy, this person wanted me to fill it at the mill. These people wanted to sell the pills at a higher rate on the street, and allowing these undocumented prescriptions to be filled for people whose names might be real of not was a way for these drug traffickers to be able to sell on the street to kids, adults that needed more pills, or even to doctors' offices as samples. At the bottom of the list was a note stating that they expected these hundred prescriptions to be filled within three days, and someone would be in touch to collect them. But where and how they would be retrieved was not stated in the note.

I had no idea what to do. I had no idea where to hide. This apothecary was my life, and its purpose was to save lives.

Unfortunately, this story has no ending right now, and my only choice seems to be to close shop and start over again under a different name in different location. Hopefully, it will be a mail order pharmacy where no one knows my name, and no one knows where I came from. My name is MD, and this is not the end of my story.

Confined!

TERRIFIED TO LEAVE HER HOUSE

FERN:

The walls are closing in around me. I am suffocating and cannot catch my breath. No one can hear my screams. I have buried myself under the couch for fear that this deadly virus will find me.

My windows are boarded up, and I can no longer see the trees, the sunshine, or anything. I made sure that no air can get through by taping and cementing the windowsills, the sides, and even my door, making sure that no draft can come in from the hallways.

This virus has many people in the hospital, others not leaving their homes except to get food or medicine.

I have stockpiled paper goods all my life. I have at least five hundred rolls of toilet paper on my floor and five hundred more in my closet, plus about four hundred cases of paper towels in the basement. There are also a thousand packages of napkins, paper plates, five hundred cans of soup, tuna cans, coffee pods, spaghetti, sauce, and lots of meat in the freezer. I even froze some rolls and some bagels.

The indoor compactor sends my trash down the chute. In order to get food, I have managed to create a special chute in my basement which opens to the outside, and has a small platform and a basket attached to it so the delivery person can just drop the bag into the chute, making sure they are wearing protective gloves. But I know I must sanitize the packages without touching the bags, which are paper, not plastic—at my request. Anything cardboard just stays on the floor for several days.

I have sanitizers, wipes, and lots of gloves to protect myself from this virus. I am afraid to go outside. I am so scared, and although I am confined to my house and my living room or bedroom, this house has lots of rooms. I have lots of space, but it is still like being behind bars in a prison. At first it was not so bad, but suddenly, I've begun feeling tired with a stuffy nose, and worst of all I have developed a hacking cough.

I cannot escape and I am feeling trapped. Crying, screaming, lashing out at myself, freezing up and trying the knobs on my doors to get out, I am terrified. Suddenly, I realize that I can no longer leave my prison that I have created for myself. My doors are made of steel like that of a bank vault. My pulse is racing, and no one can hear my screams.

My walls are soundproof, so my neighbors never really know if I am home or not. Different thoughts are going through my mind as I manage to reach for the remote on my television to see what is happening in the world, to see if by some miracle this virus is gone. But the number of deaths has increased.

I am sweating and have no way out. I check all my windows, but I really taped them shut, and even cemented the sills so that they cannot open. My only hope is the window in the bathroom. I am hoping that since it is up so high, I might be able to reach it with something to break it open, so maybe people can hear me and save me from myself.

My heart is beating fast. I can feel that my temperature is rising, and my face is burning hot. My legs feel like lead, and the chills are running through me. The hacking cough is worse, and I can barely catch my breath. What is this that attacked? Listening to the news and hearing about this horrendous virus, I realize that I might be a victim of it too.

Last night I saw on the news that one of my neighbors was hospitalized with this virus, and her breathing was poor, and they had to put her on a ventilator. How am I going to get help when I have been confined to this room for so long and have no idea how I am going to survive?

The final verdict is out, and you should learn one thing from reading this story—never isolate yourself from the world. Never be afraid of connecting with neighbors, and never feel so paranoid that you cannot deal with the outside world.

By locking yourself in not only is your body confined, but so is your mind.

What finally happens to her? Fern is still a captive of her own fears, but she decided to begin a release and hoped that by opening one window shade just a crack she would begin to see the sunlight. She did, but the reflection facing her in the window was hers.

Journey to Nowhere

All I had with me was my suitcase and the clothes on my back. I looked straight ahead of me and saw an endless dirt road which extended for miles and miles. Wearing my lucky old beat up hat and my woolen coat, I left home early that morning to decide my fate.

My day had begun with breakfast, going to work at the bank, and coming home to an all but empty apartment with just my faithful dog for company. I felt as though I was going through the motions of life, and my life resembled watching an old movie or rerun of a television program every day.

Life became mundane, with no challenges ahead and nothing to look forward to. I got up at the same time every day, went to work, and came home. I was a bank president of the largest bank in this town. It was not a very exciting job, but the money was good and it paid for my kids' school tuition fees and their various extra-curricular activities. There was even money for my soon to be ex-wife to shop wherever and whenever she wanted.

My wife, who never had to work a day in her life, said she was bored, and I provided her with no excitement. She had been going to the gym, working out, and met someone else there. She decided to take herself and my children and go and live with this total stranger after knowing him for just one month. She even managed to get herself a job as a copy editor at the local newspaper in the area where she was moving to. The man she'd met was the paper's editor, and I could not see how his job was any more exciting than mine was. However, he was ten years younger than me, and that seemed to be the draw.

Watching them leave and feeling a tangled mixture of emotions, I realized that I could not make a difference in other people's lives. I needed to start with my own. Staring into her new paramour's face as he got into his car with my family, I had an uneasy feeling. His eyes stared straight at me and his smile was cold and frightening. He looked evil. He did not speak directly to me, and my kids were shaking with fear. My wife told me it would be better this way, and she got into the car and never looked back.

I stood there staring at the back of the car until it disappeared. I could not believe what had happened, nor would I ever believe that I had no choice but to let it. My children were my life, and I could not think about living the rest of it without them. However, Jana felt that since I bored her to death with being at the bank all day, and nothing much ever happened to excite her day, this young guy whose face looked cold and demonic was the right one for her. It was as if he had her under a spell.

I began to think of places I could go and where I would spend the rest of my life. I could not even think that far ahead. I wandered down the road until I came to a small body of water surrounded by trees and grass. There was no one in sight. It was pitch black. The sky was covered with clouds so dark and ominous that I stood frozen to the spot and could not move. The air was damp and yet I felt nothing. I was neither hot nor cold. I felt numb. Feeling nothing but the pain in my heart and fear that someone would finally find me and make me go back to the life I had before, I knew that I had to make a move in some direction.

I began contemplating my next step. I did not know where I was or where the road would lead me. It was so dark that I decided to stay where I was until morning. However, that decision was not so easy to fulfill. I saw a light coming towards me from a distance. I hid behind a tree—or at least I tried to—but I was wearing a yellow shirt and the driver must have seen me from a distance. He got out and walked in my direction. Being in an isolated area, I did not know where to go or where to run. I just stood there like a statue hoping I would look like part of the scenery.

As he came closer, I realized he was a police officer and might recognize me and take me back home. He drew closer, but before he could approach close enough to speak I heard the crackling of his radio, and he stopped in his tracks, but not before looking me straight in the eye with his cold eyes and icy stare. His smile sent chills down my spine, and I prayed he would not come any closer.

Suddenly he turned and returned to his car, and I breathed a huge sigh of relief. I had thought for a minute that he was the man who had taken my family away from me. However, from a distance, I could not be sure.

I passed the night in that place, rooted to the spot, afraid and unsure of myself. With the coming of daylight, I summoned what remained of my courage, and made my way home. That very day, things began to change.

My head began to hurt, and I could not see where I was going. I had just been to the eye doctor, who had given me a new prescription for distance glasses. He assured me that wearing them would make things look much clearer. The glasses would help me not only see where I was, but also, possibly, where I needed to go. That remark seemed strange at the time, but I passed it off as him trying to make me feel better. Little did I know things would change radically for me, and I would have no idea how or why.

Putting on the new glasses I began walking, with no idea where I might end up. After walking for over an hour I came to what I thought was a small town. Everything in the town was new and in pristine condition. All the people were older, and looked like they were going about their business without noticing or stopping to speak with anyone who came their way. Everyone was dressed alike, everyone looked alike, and yet no one said a word. All the stores were well kept but had no customers in them. All of them had one person standing at a cash register waiting to check out an order, but no one entered any of the stores.

I began adjusting my glasses to make sure that I was seeing clearly when someone tapped me on the shoulder.

"Why aren't you in your proper place, and why are you just wandering around doing nothing? Don't you know that is not the way we do things here? Haven't you been here long enough?"

The man did not introduce himself, nor did he stop to hear my response. He just kept on going, saying the same thing. "There is no hope for our young people today. So irresponsible, so undependable, and so worthless."

I walked a little further, stopped, and stared at myself in a store window. Staring back at me was a younger man dressed like all the other people in this town, but it was me, looking at least ten years younger. It seemed that the man had known who I was, or at least he was pretending to know me, but he never called me by name nor told me where I was, or what he thought I was supposed to be doing.

The entire town was about ten blocks long and five blocks wide. Each block had three or four stores and three or four small houses. Behind each of the stores were wooded areas, and behind that were what looked like gated communities. No one seemed to notice or care that I was there, except for the one person.

As I came to the end of the town, I could not believe what I saw. A sign read:

You are leaving the town of
MUNDANE AND NO EXCITEMENT
Today's date is January 25, 2025

What had happened to me in between? When I left home, it was 2010. Where had fifteen years gone, and where was I during those years?

Walking out of the town, I came to a fork in the road with four signs. The first one read:

The road to the town of
NOWHERE
Keep wandering

The second read:

The road to the town of
DECISIONS

The third announced itself as:

The road to the town of
SURPRISES

And the fourth said:

JUST WALK IN THIS DIRECTION
AND YOU WILL FIND OUT...

I had no idea what these signs really meant, and since I was really nowhere that I knew, I thought about taking off my glasses and hoping to find myself back where I'd started and in my own hometown. However, when I did, nothing changed. I started walking in the direction of the second town, hoping that this town of Decisions would help me make some for myself. However, when I got there, I knew things were only going to get worse.

Facing me at the entrance of the town was the man who had taken my family. Facing me with his cold stare and chalky face, he stood there all alone and smiled.

"Where are my kids and Jana?" I asked.

He just stared at me as if I were invisible, and then vanished into thin air. I looked around and saw nothing. I looked straight ahead of me where he had been standing, and I saw something so frightening that I thought I might be hallucinating—a vision. I could see what looked like a floating ball, and inside the ball, I could see my family.

However, they were no longer my family—they were now his. Each one had been transformed into a carbon copy of this demonic creature. Each sat on a chair or bed staring into space with a strange grin on his/her face. Just blank stares. They were under a spell or drugged. Then the vision disappeared.

Frightened to think or even move, I just stood where I was and took off my glasses. I began looking around and saw that I was no longer in the town, but on the same road I was walking on when I left home.

I sat down in the middle of road and started to cry. Where was I, and what was happening?

Suddenly, I heard voices and loud yells and screams. "Happy New Year! It is now the year 2200, and what a great world it is. Welcome to the next century."

Where had the time gone? I had just been in the year 2025. It seemed every time I left a place I was sent even further into the future.

I might be on the same road that I'd started my journey on, but my surroundings were different. Instead of the beautiful houses and trees in the once countrified community that I had lived in, the area was totally devoid of any trees, vegetation, or houses. The road was no longer paved. It was constructed from hard stones and pebbles. The surrounding area featured burnt out barns and houses that were in total disrepair.

I walked along this road hoping to find a small town or any sign of people. What I did find was so frightening I stood there and froze.

In front of me was a community of small children who looked like they were all alone, with no adults in sight. They seemed to be part of some colony. The oldest of these children looked to be about sixteen. The rest of the children were lined up in front of me, and one other person that looked about eighteen seemed to be in charge. The date was January 25, 2200.

"Everyone here has a job to do. You will follow our orders. If you disobey, you will be severely punished. None of your parents survived the fire and the attack on this village. You have no other place to go. Everyone here must band together and try to make this place our home. You will have chores to do and some studies that we decide you must learn.

"You will also cook and clean for yourselves. Hunting and gathering food are your job if you want to eat and stay alive. There are no more supermarkets, restaurants, or even convenience stores. We do have a small general store where our small community can get certain things that we need. However, there are many animals that you can kill and hunt down and eat. We are lucky to have several cows that can be milked and some hens that might lay some eggs.

"You are here, and that is all there is to it. Everyone must get to work to build a shelter to live in, or use whatever houses are here. You can rebuild something or just start from scratch. I do not care. Just remember, we are a community, and we must stick together and protect ourselves from any strangers from any other villages or cities that might try and come here and take what little we have."

Just as he was about to turn back and go into what appeared to be a small house, he saw me standing there looking straight into his cold eyes.

I could not believe it. The face that was staring straight at me was a younger version of the man who had taken my family away so many years ago. This person must be his son or grandson. I froze where I was standing. However, he said nothing. Maybe they could not see me clearly, but I could see them.

How could the future of the world turn into what looked like the past? As I was propelled into the future, it felt like the world was moving backwards in time.

As I stood watching the scene before me someone must have come up from behind, hit me on the head with something hard, and knocked me out cold.

When I finally woke up, I had a throbbing headache, felt nauseous, and could barely sit up. The left side of my face and head were covered in dried blood. Whatever I was knocked out with had had a sharp edge, and really did some major damage to my head and my face. I could not stand up without feeling dizzy and light-headed. I did not see anyone around. My eyes were having trouble focusing on where I was, and my vision was blurry. What had happened to the village and the community where I saw the strange man?

When my vision finally cleared and the throbbing in my head seemed to be subsiding, I took a long look at my surroundings. I was no longer in the same place I was before I was knocked out. I was in an open field with nothing but grass and farmland in the distance. I could not see any barns, or farmhouses, or anything. There was no one in sight as far as I could see.

When I was finally able to stand up, I knew I needed to decide which way to go. Where should I walk and in what direction? However, all I saw on all four sides were empty fields of green for miles around. Then out of nowhere, I saw an object coming at me at a high speed from a distance. I tried to get out of its way, but I had no idea what it was or who was controlling it.

In a flash and a blur someone grabbed my arms and my legs, I was thrown into a vehicle, and something was placed over my head. I could not see anything at all. I tried to scream but nothing came out of my mouth. My screams fell on deaf ears.

After what seemed like an age the vehicle stopped, and when I was finally taken out of the vehicle and my eyes uncovered, I was no longer in the village with the children, nor was I in the town of Boredom and Mundane. This was somewhere else. People were standing on moving sidewalks, and cars of sorts were going at warp speeds high in the air, flying over other layers of traffic. There were people on phones who were able to not only talk to the person, but see them as well. The stores and the shops' clerks and managers did not look human—they looked like droids of some kind.

The people had odd stares and their faces seemed fixed with one expression. No one noticed me or seemed to realize that I was different. Hanging in mid-air was a calendar that said, Today is January 25, the year is 3000. It will be warm and sunny today just like yesterday and tomorrow. The temperature will be 75 degrees today, just like yesterday and tomorrow. The name of this town is Stand Still.

I began to rethink what had happened to me so far, and realized that in every place I had been the date was the same, but the year changed each time.

Just as I was about to try and leave this town, I saw standing right in front of me the demonic face and cold stare of a young man who seemed frozen in time. He had not aged at all. His appearance was the same as it was when he came and took my family away from me. Behind him were my Jana and my children, all looking straight at me with that, same cold stare and drugged smile.

As I stood, uncomprehending and afraid, a voice from somewhere in my dim memory spoke softly from the deepest recesses of my mind.

"Welcome to Your Life. The places might change, the date will stay the same, and the GLASSES will determine what happens to you. I am the eye doctor—do you see things clearly now?"

The Supermarket

There was no more public transportation as a result of the last pandemic. Cars and car services were the only transportation we had, at least in the state where I lived. The state did not want to pay for keeping the trains and buses sanitized and cleaned overnight, and paying workers time and a half. They would rather put the money into other things like the economy, recreational activities, hopefully the schools. And from now on parents had to drive their children to school and pick them up, as school buses were no longer allowed on the streets.

The world as we now knew it was bleak, and I realized that I'd really never appreciated the trains, the buses, and even the planes that helped us get from place to place. I guess we all took them for granted. Planes were allowed, but they limited the number of passengers because social distancing was the way of the world from now on, and the government had even established companies that made the required masks and gloves everyone had to wear when outdoors.

I was going to my local deli and then to the supermarket to hopefully get some deli meat for sandwiches, bread, peanut butter, jelly, butter, cream cheese, and milk. At the supermarket they would hopefully have lots of choices of food neatly protected and wrapped the right way, including fruits and vegetables that were fresh, and canned foods. The deli did not limit the amount you could buy, but the supermarket did. One person could get up to five packages of meat, two pounds of tuna, chicken salad, egg salad, and other salads, and as far as paper goods only one to every customer of each kind. So, families had to be creative and shop at the same time but not together, so when you stood in line you could get more of everything as if you were there alone and not with anyone else.

The atmosphere in the deli was warm and friendly, as the owner was thrilled to have regular customers. The supermarket had a guard at the door making sure customers followed the rules by wearing a mask, gloves, or using the sanitizer they provided. Walking around was so quiet and eerie. No one smiled, no one said hello—everyone was in a hurry to make their purchases and leave. The hardest part was finding certain items, and no one in the supermarket would help. The staff stocked items, but did not stop to say good morning or offer help. The customer service area had someone, but she was never that forthcoming, and looked annoyed if questioned.

Walking around, I found paper goods, a limited supply of trash bags, no masks, and very few items in the pharmacy department, so I had to settle for Tylenol because they had no ibuprofen or aspirin. Hoping they did not realize that my daughter was with me, we managed to get most of what was on the list and leave, but not together. I had even parked my car out of site of the entrance of the market.

But what we had missed were the cameras all over the parking lot, and as we were about to drive away, we were stopped by security and taken into custody. It was against the law to get double of anything, and even when I explained our situation, and that my son needed certain foods for health reasons and that my wife needed sugar free foods because she was diabetic, they did not care. Offering to pay extra did not work, and in the long run we had to return some of the foods and were lucky not to be fined. We were also banned for two weeks from shopping there, and our pass cards to shop were taken away.

This was a horrible world to live in, and within the two weeks we were lucky that the deli got us certain foods. Neighbors would never share, and my wife wound up in the hospital because of her low blood sugar and more.

The hospital did just so much, and the medical care at that time did not always cover certain tests in the emergency room unless your primary doctor approved them. But, since this event happened because of an infraction of the rules established by the state government, we were lucky to be allowed to get any help at all. Horrible, to say the least, that people had to suffer, and others would lose their lives because a few who wanted for nothing set the rules.

***

A neighboring family went to their local supermarket and wanted to buy extra baby food for their twin girls. How could these infants share one jar of apple sauce, one jar of peas, and one jar of mixed vegetables? The parents were not even allowed to buy enough formula for both twins. Something had to be done—and someone had to take charge and defend the people. But who would stand up to the state government, and who would back this person when push came to shove?

Danny and his wife Jill were the ones whose twins were malnourished because of this ridiculous rationing rule, when the surplus was there and the amount of food in the markets was not diminished. Someone decided that just in case of another pandemic, they wanted to make sure there was enough food to go around, even though deliveries were coming on a regular basis.

The governor was a sadistic man named Toddler, and his wife was a rich woman who spent more than he made as governor. His mansion had servants and help, and enough food stocked and stored to last for years. He couldn't care less about his constituents. The police were in his hip pocket and wanted for nothing. This governor was corrupt and into other areas, even helping the drug cartels sell to pill mills and street sellers.

Even though people knew what he was doing, no one dared to say anything for fear of the police learning about it. Not only did they have cameras everywhere, hidden microphones in every store, and video tapes with sound, the police could also be wearing hidden mics on their uniforms, and could hear and record every word.

Someone needed to run against him in the upcoming election. But who?

Shaun Brown was a smart kid whose father was an IT man, and Shaun had an idea to take this governor down. With links to some powerful businessmen, his father hoped to get the backing to take down the governor and anyone that was corrupt in the police department.

Toddler was smart, and began with a smear campaign about Brown's business practices, making claims that he hacked into government websites, was linked to a cartel that sold drugs, and other lies about his relationships with different women.

Brown answered every accusation, and the public started to rise to his calling, especially those that felt oppressed in their jobs, those that wanted more out of life other than being allowed to go to the market once a week, food rationing, and the decline in the educational system, and Toddler's new surcharge on prescription drugs above and beyond the normal co-payments. People were starting to rise up, but the problem was, would they come out and vote?

Toddler sent out emails and threatening letters, and dared anyone to vote against him. He did not care about the people in his state—he only cared about control, making sure he and his cohorts had food, supplies, places to eat, and expensive cars. He even charged protection money to small businesses in order for them to remain open.

Election day was just a few days away, and the polls were in favor of Toddler eighty-five to fifteen. People were afraid. People wanted change, but would they stand up and be counted in the right direction?

This state had exactly, according to their census bureau, five thousand people that were eligible to vote. Toddler did not even need a majority. He just needed to have more votes.

Election day came and the voters were not in booths. They voted online on a special website which handled votes and counted them. At the end of the day the tally was shocking.

Toddler: 2499
Brown: 2499

Tied!

Each candidated only needed one more vote to be victorious, but where would it come from?

A total of 4998 votes meant two people hadn't voted. One had died the day before, leaving one person, you, to decide who will win.

Which kind of society do you want to live in — Toddler's or Brown's?